Sir BORIS the BRAVE
and the Tall Tales Princess

Marc Starbuck ✳ **Becka Moor**

EGMONT

Sir **Boris** the **Brave** is the boldest, bravest and busiest **knight** in all the land.

He topples **trolls**,

SIR BORIS

jousts **giants**,

saves **cities**

SIR BORIS
SAVES THE DAY...
AGAIN

OUR HERO

and wins *Knight of the Realm* every year!

SIR
BORIS
no.1

One day, Sir Boris was scraping a very pongy piece of goblin poo from his shoe when an urgent message arrived.

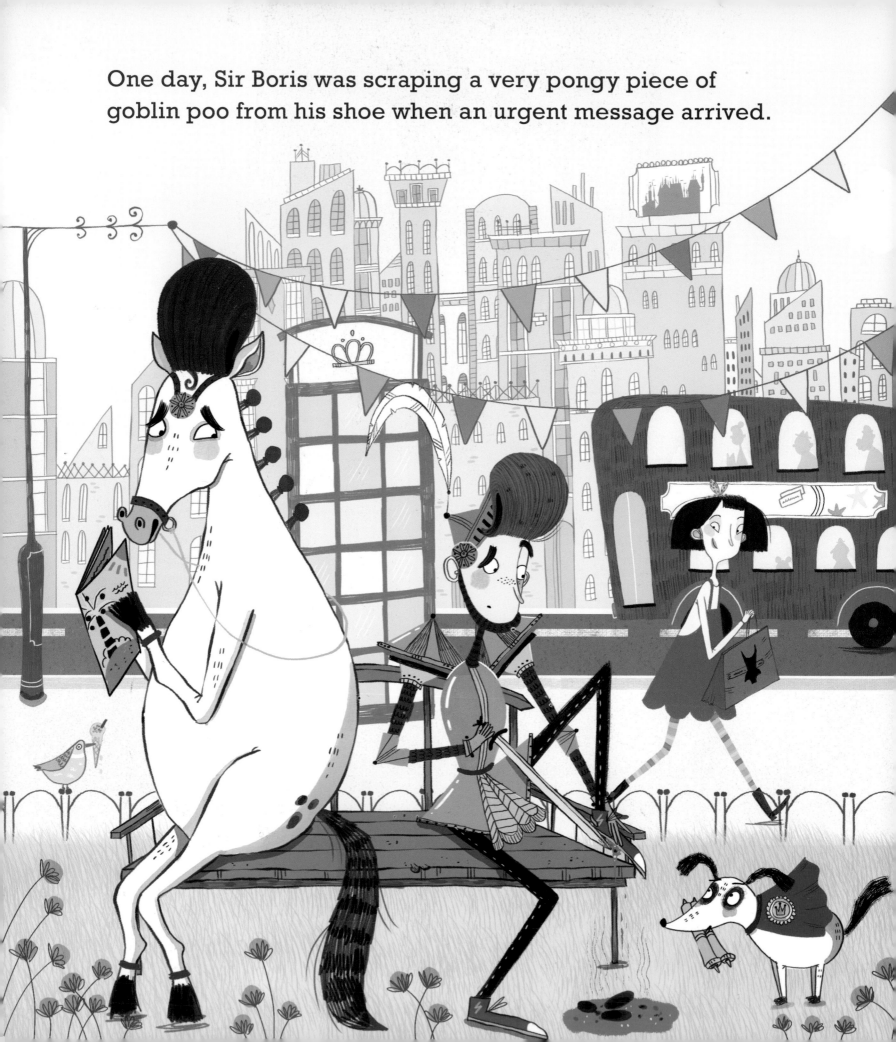

Dear Sir Boris the Brave,
Help! I am being held prisoner by a ghastly **ogre**. I am in need of immediate rescue. **This is an emergency!**
Kind regards,
Princess Tilly Talltales

P.S. All visitors must bring me a gift.
Make it sparkly!

So Sir Boris grabbed his trusty sword and shield and galloped gallantly to the rescue.

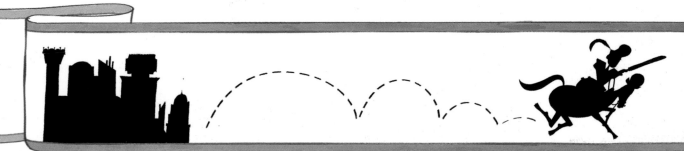

"Sir Boris the Brave to the rescue!" bellowed the famous knight as he whooshed through the palace window.

Princess Tilly Talltales tapped her watch impatiently. "And about time too!" she whined. "That ghastly ogre won't let me play with my friends until I've tidied my room. It's just not fair!"

"I am not an ogre. **I am the king**," grumbled the king.

Sir Boris was shocked. "Your room is a mess and this IS NOT an emergency," he said sternly.

"It **is** an emergency,"

shrieked the princess.

"I'm bored!"

"Princess Tilly Talltales," sighed Sir Boris. "You must only call for help when it is a real emergency. Now tidy up and stop being so silly."

The next day, Sir Boris was spraying slithery snake slime from his shield when another urgent message arrived.

Dear Sir Boris the Brave,

Help!
I am being picked on by a wicked old **witch**. This is **definitely** an emergency so saddle up and get galloping!

Kind regards,
Princess Tilly Talltales

P.S. Also, I really, really need some chocolate.

So Sir Boris grabbed his trusty sword and shield and got galloping.

"Sir Boris the Brave to the **rescue!**" bellowed the fearless knight, as he burst through the palace gates.

Princess Tilly Talltales scowled at him and pointed, "That **wicked old** witch won't buy me a new dress and I haven't got a thing to wear!"

"I am not a witch. I am the **queen,**" groaned the queen.

Sir Boris took a very, very deep breath.

"This is definitely **not** an emergency," he sighed.

"IT IS!"
cried the princess.
"I cannot be seen
wearing the
same dress twice!"

"Princess Tilly Talltales," said Sir Boris, "I've told you before. You must **only** call for help when it is a **real emergency.** Now, wear one of these delightful dresses – I'm thinking pastels – and stop being so silly."

A few days later, after an unfortunate incident with a flu-ridden giant, yet another urgent message arrived.

Dear Sir **Boris** the Brave,
HELP! A horrid, hairy
beast
is loose in the palace.
Bring your **sharpest**
sword and stop reading
this urgent message.
This is absolutely,
definitely an
emergency!

Kind regards,
Princess Tilly Talltales

P.S. Why, why,
why don't
you have
a phone?

Well, the princess must really be in trouble
this time, thought Sir Boris, so he grabbed
his trusty sword and shield . . .

"Sir Boris the Brave to the rescue!" bellowed the dashing knight as he swooped across the ballroom on a sparkly chandelier.

Princess Tilly Talltales angrily stamped her foot.

"That horrid, hairy beast is going to eat me," she screeched. **"Off with its head!"**

"Eeek!" squeaked the hairy beast.

Sir Boris had heard enough.

"This is **absolutely, definitely**, not an emergency!" he snapped. "And that is not a hairy beast. It is a mouse called Edward."

"A mouse!" screamed the princess.

"Princess Tilly Talltales, for the final time," declared Sir Boris.
"You must only call for help when it is a **real emergency**.

Now fetch Edward your finest chunk
of cheese and stop being so silly."

The following morning, Sir Boris the Brave
was enjoying a much needed rest, when
another urgent
message arrived.

Dear Sir Boris the Brave,
Help! A horrible,
hungry dragon
is going to eat me.
Come at once.
Preferably a lot quicker
than you did the
last three times.
Hurry!

Kind regards, Princess Tilly Talltales

P.S. This is a REAL emergency!

"A dragon now, is it?" snorted Sir Boris.
"Whatever will she think of next?"

Then Sir Boris the Brave did something
that he had **never**, ever done before . . .

. . . he took the **day off**

and went to the seaside!

Where he had a bit of bother in a boat and was rescued by a fair maiden.

They fell in **love!**

And lived happily ever after, toppling trolls, jousting giants, saving cities and galloping gallantly to real emergencies.

As for **Princess Tilly Talltales** . . .

. . . well, she never bothered Sir Boris the Brave ever again!